P9-BZY-683

Piglets Don't Watch Television

by Trina Wiebe

Illustrations
by Marisol Sarrazin

To my husband, Andy, for his endless patience and unwavering faith in me.

Published in 2007 by Lobster Press™
1620 Sherbrooke St. West, Suites C & D
Montréal, Québec H3H 1C9
Tel. (514) 904-1100 • Fax (514) 904-1101
www.lobsterpress.com • www.abbyandtess.com

Publisher: Alison Fripp
Editor: Jane Pavanel
Cover design: Marielle Maheu
Inside design: Geneviève Mayers
Production Manager: Tammy Desnoyers

We acknowledge the financial support of the Government of Canada through the Book Publishing Industry Development Program (BPIDP) for our publishing activities.

We acknowledge the support of the Canada Council for the Arts for our publishing program.

Canadian Cataloguing in Publication Data
Wiebe, Trina, 1970-
(Abby and Tess, Pet-Sitters™; 3)
ISBN 978-1-894222-16-7

I. Sarrazin, Marisol, 1965- II. Title.
III. Series: Wiebe, Trina, 1970- Abby and Tess, Pet-Sitters™; 3.

PS8595.I358P53 2000 jC813'.6 C00-900845-4
PZ7.W6349Pi 2000

Printed and bound in the United States.

Contents

1 A Normal Pet

"I'll get it," yelled Abby as she raced down the hall to the kitchen.

The phone rang again before Abby could pick it up. "Hello?" she said, out of breath.

"Yes, hello," said a woman's voice into her ear. "May I speak to Abby or Tess please?"

Abby's heart leapt. This might be the call she'd been waiting for. It had been weeks since anyone had called about a job.

"I'm Abby," she said, trying to contain her excitement.

"My name is Ms. Fitzpatrick. I saw your poster in Jeremy Nakama's pet store. You're a pet-sitter, right?"

Abby did a little dance. It *was* the call she'd been waiting for. "Yes, I am," she said in her best professional voice. "My little sister and I are very experienced pet-sitters. What can we do for you?"

Abby had practiced these words again

and again in front of the bathroom mirror. She'd wanted to sound grown-up and business-like when people called. Clients needed to know they were leaving their pets in good hands when they went away. And every word was completely true. She and Tess had loads of experience pet-sitting. They'd taken care of two squeaky-clean goldfish and an ornery lizard. They could handle anything.

"Well," said Ms. Fitzpatrick, "I have an out-of-town seminar to attend and I'll be gone for three days. I really don't want to leave Prissy by herself because she tends to get lonely."

There was a clunking sound on the other end of the line, then a series of short barks. Ms. Fitzpatrick laughed. "Okay, Prissy, Mommy will be off the phone in just a moment."

To Abby she said, "I need someone to feed her every day and keep her company. Are you interested in the job?"

Abby grinned. Was she ever! "Yes, certainly," she replied. "Just tell me when and where."

Abby scribbled down the address and meeting time and thanked Ms. Fitzpatrick politely. Then she hung up the phone and let out a whoop. A job! Just wait until she told Tess!

She knew Tess would be thrilled too. She loved animals almost as much as Abby did, which was why they'd started their pet-sitting business in the first place. That, plus the fact that the apartment building they lived in didn't allow animals. Abby thought the No Pets Allowed rule was stupid, but it didn't bother her so much now that they were looking after other people's pets.

Abby raced down the hall to the bedroom she shared with Tess. She flung open the door. On her side of the room there was a tidy bed, a neatly organized desk and a shelf full of animal books. On Tess's side the bed was rumpled, the toy box was half empty and the wooden dresser had most of its drawers hanging out.

"Tess," shouted Abby. "I've got great news!"

"Woof!" Tess was bent over with her back to the closet. She was vigorously scooping up toys and dirty clothes and trying to propel them between her legs through the open door. She looked like a dog digging a hole for a bone, only instead of dirt flying everywhere, it was socks and underwear.

Abby stared at the mess. "What are you doing?"

Tess paused in her work and looked up at her sister. "Mom said I had to clean up before I could watch cartoons. So I'm cleaning up."

Abby sighed. Tess was a little unusual. She barked at strangers and howled when she was upset. She liked to carry the Saturday newspaper around the apartment in her teeth. Sometimes she even thought she had fleas. Her behavior used to bug Abby, but it didn't anymore. Well . . . most of the time, anyway.

"Why are you doing it that way?" she said, shaking her head. Not all of Tess's things had actually made it into the closet. Some were flung around the room, leaving it almost as

messy as before. "It doesn't make any sense. You'd be done in half the time if you just did it properly."

"Who was on the phone?" Tess asked, deliberately changing the subject.

"Oh, yeah," said Abby, brightening up. "We've got another pet-sitting job! For three whole days!"

Tess sat back on her haunches and stared up at Abby. "Really?"

Abby nodded. "I said we'd go over tomorrow after school."

Tess yipped happily. "What kind of animal is it?"

"A dog," Abby said. "I heard it barking in the background when Ms. Fitzpatrick was talking to me. She called it Prissy."

"A dog?" breathed Tess. Her eyes grew wide. They had never pet-sat a dog before. "Really?"

"Yup," said Abby. "Isn't it awesome? We finally get to look after a normal pet!"

2 Perfect for the Job

Abby and Tess had no trouble finding their way to Ms. Fitzpatrick's the next day. Abby's best friend, Rachel, lived in the same neighborhood and Abby had been there many times.

Ms. Fitzpatrick's house was big and had lots of gleaming windows. Along the front was a large covered porch holding fancy wicker furniture. White curlycue trim made a lacy pattern along the roofline and delicate green ivy crept up the walls.

"It looks like a picture from a magazine, doesn't it?" whispered Abby as they approached the front door.

"Woof," agreed Tess, staring at the potted geraniums that were evenly spaced along the porch railing.

They climbed the stairs and Abby rang the bell. Ms. Fitzpatrick opened the front door. She wore a sensible gray suit made of a smooth, shiny fabric. Her hair hung to her shoulders in a no-nonsense cut. She smiled at the girls.

"Hello," she said briskly. "You're right on time. Won't you please come in." It didn't sound like a question. Ms. Fitzpatrick seemed like the kind of person who was used to giving orders.

Abby and Tess stepped inside and immediately heard several short, sharp barks from deep within the house. Ms. Fitzpatrick turned and called out, "Prissy! Stop that right now. Be a good girl." There was a clattering noise and the barking stopped.

She led them into the living room, which was filled with large, expensive-looking furniture. There were plants everywhere, many of them in bloom. Abby recognized only one, a furry purple African violet that was just like a plant Mom had at home.

"Please sit down," Ms. Fitzpatrick instructed.

Abby looked at the sofa. It was covered with toys. She glanced around the room and noticed there were toys all over the place. She wondered how many kids lived in the house. There must be a lot. She and Tess combined didn't have this many toys!

She pushed aside a half-dressed baby doll and some large plastic stacking blocks, then sat in the cleared spot. Tess squeezed in beside her.

"I'll be gone for three days," Ms. Fitzpatrick began, sitting down opposite them. "Starting tomorrow. That's Saturday, Sunday and Monday. Will that be okay?"

"We get Monday off," Abby assured her

quickly. "It's a teacher development day."

Ms. Fitzpatrick nodded and drummed her fingers on the arm of her chair. "Good. That works out well for me. Prissy needs to be fed and groomed, but I also want you to provide companionship. She gets terribly lonely when I'm away. I'd like you to spend an hour playing with her each morning. I'll pay you well, of course."

Abby smiled. That sounded pretty good.

"Prissy hates going to the kennel. It's so hard on her to be in a strange place with people who don't really care about her. The last time she went to the kennel she was upset for days afterwards. I'm hoping this arrangement will be easier for her."

"We'll do our best," Abby said.

"Yes, of course," Ms. Fitzpatrick replied. She paused, fixing her gaze on Abby. "Somehow I expected you to be older. You do have experience with this sort of thing?"

Abby nodded emphatically. "Oh, yes. We've taken care of all kinds of animals. We're perfect for the job." She glanced at Tess, hoping she wouldn't blurt out that they'd only looked after goldfish and a lizard.

Ms. Fitzpatrick seemed to make up her mind. "Good," she said, standing up and smoothing her skirt with her hands. "Let's go find Prissy and see what she thinks. Follow me."

Abby and Tess rose obediently and fell into step behind her. They had to pick their way carefully to avoid tripping on the rubber balls and plastic bowling pins that lay about.

"I wonder what kind of dog it is," Abby whispered to Tess behind Ms. Fitzpatrick's back.

Tess hopped over a yellow rubber ducky, narrowly missing a dump truck. "I wish I had this many toys," she whispered back. "Mom never lets me make a mess like this."

Abby waved at Tess to be quiet. But she did have a point, Abby thought, glancing around. Ms. Fitzpatrick's kids must be pretty spoiled.

Finally they entered the kitchen. It was empty, though there were more toys and signs of Prissy everywhere. On the floor under the table lay a rubber squeaky toy shaped like a banana.

A pink leash was looped over the back of a chair. And food and water dishes sat side by side on the floor next to a set of glass garden doors.

Through the doors Abby and Tess could see more toys in the backyard. Under a big tree was a purple plastic wading pool surrounded by colorful inflatable beach toys.

But the yard was empty too.

"Where are your kids?" Tess asked, speaking up for the first time.

"Kids?" Ms. Fitzpatrick sounded surprised. "I don't have any children. My work as a computer programmer is very demanding and I travel a lot. It's just me and Prissy, which is why I need someone to keep her company this weekend."

Abby raised her eyebrows. No kids? Then all these toys must belong to the dog. Talk about spoiled!

Ms. Fitzpatrick crossed the kitchen and stood at the entrance to a long hallway. "Prissy?" she called. "Come here, sweetie. You have guests."

3 A Surprising Twist

"Prissy," called Ms. Fitzpatrick again. "Mommy's got a treat for you." Tess grabbed Abby's hand, urging her forward. They peered around Ms. Fitzpatrick, hoping to catch a glimpse of Prissy.

A moment passed. Ms. Fitzpatrick turned to the girls. "Prissy usually isn't shy. Perhaps she's taking a nap. Her room is right through here."

A dog with its own room? Abby couldn't believe it. Even she and Tess didn't have their own rooms.

"Prissy likes her privacy," Ms. Fitzpatrick explained as she led the girls down the hall. She stopped in front of a door decorated with a pretty pink bow. "She's very sensitive."

"Me too," said Abby automatically, "I mean, I like privacy too." She couldn't look at Tess. She was afraid she might start giggling.

Ms. Fitzpatrick knocked lightly on the

door and then opened it. Abby and Tess crowded in behind her, curious to see what a pet's very own bedroom would look like.

It was small, but a window with a ruffled curtain let in the sunshine and made the space feel bright and cheerful. Halfway up the pink walls was a band of rosebud wallpaper. Toys and balls and pillows were scattered here and there.

"Isn't that cute?" Ms. Fitzpatrick exclaimed. "She fell asleep. But I'm sure she won't mind if I wake her up. You're probably dying to meet her."

Tess scratched behind her left ear nervously. Abby knew how she felt. She wasn't sure what to expect either.

They watched as Ms. Fitzpatrick stepped over to a white wicker basket. Inside was a fuzzy pink and white quilt that was all scrunched up in the middle. Abby stared at it. Since when did dogs sleep under the covers?

Ms. Fitzpatrick knelt beside the basket and laid her hand gently on the quilt. "Prissy,"

she said softly. "Wake up, honey. You've got company."

There was a snort, then the blanket moved. Abby and Tess watched, eager to catch sight of the most spoiled pet in the whole world.

There was another snort, followed by a sneeze. The quilt quivered, then fell away as Prissy sat up and gave a sleepy bark.

"But . . ." stammered Abby, staring at

Prissy's round pink snout and floppy pink ears. Most of Prissy was still covered by the quilt, but Abby knew what she'd see when the rest of it came off. Four hoofed feet and a corkscrew tail.

Prissy was a pig.

4 Weirder and Weirder

Prissy barked again and Abby could have sworn she was laughing at them.

"Woof, woof," replied Tess, delighted with her new friend. "She's a pig."

"Of course," said Ms. Fitzpatrick matter-of-factly. "Priscilla is a Vietnamese pot-bellied pig. Most of them have black markings, but she doesn't. She's still just a baby, though. She'll be three months old next week."

Ms. Fitzpatrick cupped Prissy's face in both hands and brought her nose close to the pig's moist snout. "Mommy promised she'd be home for Prissy's birthday party, didn't she? Oh yes, she did. We'll have a lovely party, won't we?"

Abby didn't know what to say.

"Can I pet her?" asked Tess.

"Of course you can. Pot-bellied pigs are wonderfully affectionate. Prissy especially loves being scratched behind her ears."

Tess grinned. "Me too!"

"But she barks," sputtered Abby. "Pigs oink. They don't bark."

Ms. Fitzpatrick showed Tess exactly where Prissy liked to be scratched, then glanced up at Abby. "Prissy barks quite a bit, actually. It's her way of greeting people or getting my attention. She also grunts and honks. And if I have to scold her for being naughty, she'll even shriek."

"Sounds like Tess," muttered Abby, shaking her head. It was disappointing to see a pig when she'd expected a puppy. Pet-sitting a puppy would have been a dream come true.

"Come on, Abby," coaxed Tess, tickling Prissy under the chin. "This is fun. I'll bet she likes having her belly rubbed too."

Prissy grunted happily. As if she understood Tess's words, she rolled onto her back and wiggled her short legs in the air.

Abby couldn't help smiling. Maybe pet-sitting Prissy wouldn't be so bad after all. But it was weird. Why would a computer programmer want a pig for a pet? Ms. Fitzpatrick seemed so smart and sensible.

She looked around the room again. Along one wall stood a large wooden cupboard. Before she could ask what was inside, Ms. Fitzpatrick stepped across the room and pulled the door open.

"This is where I keep Prissy's supplies and grooming equipment," she explained.

Abby stared at the shelves. They were crammed full of moisturizers and shampoos and sunscreen and all kinds of other stuff. Abby thought of their bathroom cabinet at home. It seemed empty compared to this.

"This is Prissy's food," Ms. Fitzpatrick said, bending to touch a large bag on the bottom shelf. "The people I bought her from fed her regular pig food, not special food for miniature pigs, so now she's on a strict diet. One scoop every day. No more, no less. Of course, she's allowed all the fruits and vegetables she wants."

"She likes fruits and vegetables?" asked Abby.

"Yes, of course. They're excellent for her digestion," Ms. Fitzpatrick answered.

"Oh," said Abby. She wished she'd brought her notebook and a pencil. All she had in her backpack was a crumpled lunch bag and her smelly gym clothes. She'd been so sure Prissy was a dog. She'd memorized her dog books ages ago, but she didn't know the first thing about pigs. If only she'd been able to do some research.

"This is for the litter box," continued Ms. Fitzpatrick, pointing at a second bag. "You'll need to clean it out each morning as well."

Abby wasn't sure she'd heard right. She exchanged confused glances with Tess. Grandma Ida lived in the country and her neighbors had pigs. They ate, slept and pooped outside, or else in the barn. Only cats used litter boxes.

But there, in a corner of the room, sat a litter box. It was the kind that had sides and a top, with an opening in the front and a handle for carrying. Through the opening Abby could see a layer of gray, crumbly material covering the bottom.

This job was getting weirder by the minute.

5 Abby Surfs the Net

Back home Abby turned on the computer and connected to the Internet. She typed the words "pot-bellied pig" and clicked once. Tess jiggled on a stool next to her, bumping her arm.

"Stop moving," Abby said impatiently. "You're going to make me mess up."

Tess growled, but sat still. Together they watched the screen in front of them. It blinked, then filled with words and pictures. Abby looked at the long list of pot-bellied pig links their search engine had found.

She really knew nothing at all about pot-bellied pigs. There were no books on them in her room. And she'd been so certain Prissy was a dog, she hadn't gone to the library like she usually did when they got a pet-sitting job.

Abby loved researching animals on the Internet. To her, computers were amazing. She admired the way they stored thousands of pieces of information, always perfectly filed away, just

waiting to be retrieved. When Abby became a veterinarian, she was going to have a computer in her office.

"Wow," she said, gazing at the screen. "There are hundreds of links."

"Did you find what you were looking for?" asked Mom, giving a bubbling pot of spaghetti sauce a quick stir. She left the stove and stepped over to the computer desk. "Oh, my. I didn't realize pot-bellied pigs were such popular pets."

Abby shrugged helplessly. "I don't know

where to start."

Tess gave an impatient bark and stabbed her finger at the list. "Try this one."

Her finger landed on a link called "Patti's Pig Page." Abby groaned. Pointing blindly at the screen wasn't the most reliable research method. Abby preferred to read the whole list before deciding what to do next.

"I don't think . . ." she began.

Tess glanced up at Mom to make sure she wasn't watching, then gave Abby's chair a furtive kick. "You think too much," she complained. "It's boring."

Tess never thought things through. She liked to act first and think later, which explained why Tess was always breaking things and making mistakes. Abby was the complete opposite and proud of it.

"Okay," Abby said before Tess grabbed the mouse. She wished her sister would get lost and let her do the research alone. But saying so would just make Tess stay longer.

Abby clicked on "Patti's Pig Page" and

immediately new images began forming on the screen. The words came first, then one by one several photos popped up.

Mom laughed. "Look at that!"

An unhappy pot-bellied pig was staring at them from an old-fashioned baby buggy. A frilly bonnet was tied under its chin. Beneath the photo was the name Petunia.

Abby frowned. "That's silly."

There were other photos too. One showed Petunia in a bathing suit at the beach. In another she wore a chef's hat and was eating an apple. There was also a shot of her at a computer pretending to type.

Mom shook her head. "It does seem rather ridiculous. Why would people want to keep pigs as house pets?"

Abby thought of Ms. Fitzpatrick. Why would someone who worked with computers want to come home to a pig at the end of the day? Computers were fast and precise and logical. Pigs were the opposite: undignified and sloppy and unpredictable. It made no sense.

"I don't get it either, Mom. But Ms. Fitzpatrick treats Prissy just like a kid. A totally spoiled kid. Prissy even has her own room."

"Woof," agreed Tess. "She has a swimming pool too."

Mom raised an eyebrow. "Really? She sounds like a very lucky pig."

Abby found a link called "Exotic Pets" and clicked on it. She scanned the information quickly. There were all kinds of interesting facts. The printer was out of ink again so she rummaged through the desk drawer until she found some lined paper and a pencil.

Glancing up at the screen, she began jotting down notes. Just as she'd hoped, Tess got bored and left. Abby could hear her wander down the hall to Mom's art studio.

Abby filled four pages with her neat handwriting. Finally she put down her pencil and rubbed her eyes. Her wristwatch showed she'd been writing for over an hour. She stretched, then switched off the computer. She felt much better now that she was armed with information.

Her notes were full of useful facts. For instance, Vietnamese pot-bellied pigs had been very popular in the mid-1980s. People had paid up to $20,000 for one piglet. You could buy a new car for that! Sometimes people bought regular farm pigs by mistake and were surprised when their miniature porkers grew up to weigh over 300 pounds. Abby smiled, imagining the looks on people's faces when their piggy pets ended up weighing more than they did.

Abby had also discovered that pot-bellies were quite intelligent. More intelligent than dogs, according to the "Exotic Pets" website. But Abby found that hard to believe. If pigs were so smart, why weren't there any seeing-eye pigs or guard pigs or search-and-rescue pigs?

Abby collected her notes and stapled them together. Everything she needed to know about pot-bellied pigs was now at her fingertips. She knew their likes and dislikes, their habits, their noises, the games they liked to play . . . .

She was ready for Prissy.

6 Intruders!

Bright and early on Saturday morning Abby and Tess headed in the direction of Ms. Fitzpatrick's neighborhood. Twenty minutes later the red brick house came into sight. Abby walked faster. Now that she knew what to expect, she was really looking forward to taking care of Prissy.

Tess broke into a trot to keep up. "Will the lady be there?" she asked, panting slightly.

"Nope," Abby answered, reaching inside the collar of her T-shirt to pull out her key string. She always kept the key to their apartment safely around her neck, and today Ms. Fitzpatrick's house key hung beside it. "She said she was catching an early flight this morning. Nobody's home but Prissy."

They walked up the brick path that led to the front porch. Ms. Fitzpatrick had called it a verandah. Tess raced up the steps ahead of Abby and touched the door.

"I win," she cried, her tongue hanging out of her mouth as she tried to catch her breath.

Ignoring her, Abby opened the screen door and slipped the key into the keyhole of the heavy wooden door behind it. Immediately they heard barking from inside the house. If Abby didn't know better, she'd swear it came from a poodle or a terrier.

"Woof, woof," barked Tess in reply. She scratched at the door with one hand. "Woof!"

Prissy yipped back, the sharp sound barely muffled by the thick wood of the door. Abby rolled her eyes. A girl and a pig, both of them barking like dogs. They made a good pair.

When the door swung open Tess pushed ahead of Abby and ran straight to Prissy, who was waiting expectantly. They greeted each other like long lost friends. Abby tucked the key string into her collar and shut the door behind her. With a sigh she side-stepped Tess and Prissy, who were rolling around on the carpet, barking and grunting happily.

"Come on, you two," she said, winding her

way through an obstacle course of toys. "It's time for breakfast."

Prissy made a noise that was a cross between an oink and a honk and eagerly followed Abby to the kitchen. Giggling, Tess jumped to her feet and ran after them.

"It's almost like she understands me," Abby said with surprise. Ms. Fitzpatrick had claimed Prissy knew over fifteen different words. Abby's research had said pigs were smart, but were they that smart?

Suddenly Abby stopped dead. "Tess, did you hear something?"

Tess stumbled into Prissy, who honked with alarm and raced on ahead.

"What?"

Abby strained for the sound she thought she'd heard. Nothing. She shrugged. "Never mind. I thought I heard a voice, that's all."

Tess snorted. "You said nobody was home."

"I know." Abby started toward the kitchen. "My ears must have been playing tricks on me."

She took two more steps, then stopped. "There," she whispered fiercely. "Did you hear that?"

Tess cocked her head sideways. "I don't hear . . ."

Then they both heard it. Voices and laughter. They stared at each other in shock. Someone was in the house with them.

The voices swelled, then faded, then returned again. Tess whimpered plaintively and clutched Abby's arm. "Robbers!" she cried, her voice rising to a wail.

Abby clamped a hand over Tess's mouth. "Shhh," she hissed. "Do you want them to hear us?"

Her heart was thudding so loudly she could barely hear her own voice. They had to get out of there. Grabbing Tess by the elbow, Abby backed away from the kitchen. If only they could make it to the front door without being detected!

One step. Then another. The voices in the

kitchen continued, but were too low for Abby to make out the words. They must have broken in through the garden doors, Abby thought. Or maybe they'd pried open a window. They were probably searching for money or jewelry. What would they do if they found Abby and Tess instead?

Abby shuddered and took another step backwards. She had to get Tess out of there.

She had to call the police. She had to . . . .

Abby's foot landed on a plastic bowling pin and her legs suddenly shot out from under her. She fell back, bringing Tess down with her. Her elbow caught the edge of a small table. As it crashed to the floor, a basket of potpourri flew into the air.

Dried flower petals rained down on the girls as they lay on the floor, paralyzed with fear. The voices in the kitchen stopped.

7 A Foolish Move

A petal landed on Abby's nose. It tickled, but she was too terrified to brush it off. She stared down the hall, afraid to breathe.

Nothing happened.

"Do you think they heard us?" Tess whispered as quietly as she could.

Abby was wondering the same thing. At any moment she expected a masked robber to jump out at them. The seconds dragged by. Then she heard footsteps. They were faint at first, but as they got closer they grew louder and louder.

Abby gulped and put her arms protectively around Tess. She squeezed her eyes shut, too scared to look.

A moist snout nudged her cheek and Abby's eyes flew open. Prissy was breathing hard, blowing air out her nostrils with a forceful *HUH, HUH, HUH* sound. She left a wet spot on Abby's skin.

"Prissy!" exclaimed Tess. She threw her arms around the piglet's neck. "You're safe!"

Prissy snorted again and Abby ducked to avoid her wet snout. "Quiet, Tess, they'll hear you," she whispered frantically.

Tess cocked her head again. "I can still hear them," she whispered back.

Prissy slipped out of Tess's arms and trotted down the hall, then stopped and looked back. She seemed to be waiting for them to follow her. She snorted again and disappeared into the kitchen.

"Let's get out of here," Abby said, keeping her voice low. She struggled to her feet. "Before something really bad happens."

"We can't leave Prissy," whimpered Tess.

"Prissy will be fine," Abby said, grabbing Tess by the arm. "We're the ones in danger. C'mon, let's go!"

Tess pulled free and raced down the hall. "I'm not leaving Prissy," she cried, disappearing into the kitchen after her new friend.

Abby stared after her, dumbfounded. How

could Tess do something like this? Why didn't she ever think before she acted? She was putting them both in danger. Abby shot one last wistful look at the front door, then took a deep breath and headed toward the kitchen.

No one was there.

But the voices were louder now. Abby tiptoed to Prissy's room, but it was empty too. Mystified, she returned to the kitchen. Where had everyone gone?

Then she spotted something she hadn't noticed before. A staircase was tucked away in the far corner of the kitchen, just beyond the refrigerator. Carpeted stairs led up to the second floor, probably to the bedrooms. Had Tess and Prissy gone up there?

Abby climbed the first few steps, then paused. The voices were louder now. She could hear music too. Hesitantly, she took two more steps. Then two more. The higher she climbed, the louder the voices grew. Surely Tess wouldn't have gone up there . . . .

Abby gulped and kept climbing. Thanks

to the thick carpeting, she didn't make a sound as she crept toward the second floor. The voices grew more distinct and seemed oddly familiar. Puzzled, Abby listened intently. It was as though she recognized them from somewhere.

Warily she stepped onto the landing. Six doors lined a long hall. The closest door was open so she tiptoed toward it. Gathering her courage, she peeked inside.

A large four-poster bed filled the far end of the room. Gauzy white fabric wound around the posts and was tied in place with silky cords. A low padded footstool sat on the floor at the end of the bed.

And there on the bed, looking quite comfortable in the middle of a mountain of frilly pillows, were Tess and Prissy. They were watching television.

The voices were coming from a TV show.

8 Mousse, Not Moose

Abby groaned. Ms. Fitzpatrick must have left the set on by mistake. There were no robbers. The house wasn't being ransacked and their lives had never been in danger. Suddenly she felt foolish.

"What are you doing?" she snapped at her sister. Tess lay sprawled on her stomach, her chin propped in her hands. Prissy was stretched out beside her.

"We're watching a guy make a chocolate moose," Tess said calmly.

"What?" cried Abby. How could she lie there so nonchalantly when only a few seconds ago they'd both been frightened for their lives?

"Prissy likes it," Tess said, her eyes already back on the television screen. "But I don't know how he's going to get a moose into that little kitchen."

Abby stared at the TV. A man in an apron was whisking something in a bowl. He cracked a joke and the audience laughed. Then the show switched to a commercial and music filled the bedroom. She walked over to the television and switched it off.

It was just a dumb TV show.

Tess and Prissy glared at her. "We wanted to see the moose," objected Tess.

"It's mousse, not moose," Abby said with a sigh. "They sound the same, but . . . never mind,

I'll explain later. C'mon, we need to give Prissy her breakfast."

At the sound of the word "breakfast" Prissy trotted to the end of the bed and climbed down, using the small footstool to reach the floor. She made a beeline for the stairs. Maybe she did understand, Abby thought to herself. She and Tess followed her to the kitchen.

"Why don't you measure out the dried food," Abby suggested. "I'll see what looks good in the fridge."

"Woof!" said Tess agreeably, heading for Prissy's room.

"Make sure it's exactly one scoop," called Abby. She glanced at Prissy, who was waiting patiently at her food dish. Her back curved slightly with the weight of her belly. "Doctor's orders," Abby smiled at the pig.

Prissy grunted hungrily.

"Yeah, yeah, I know." Abby poked her head into the fridge. "What would a pig enjoy for breakfast?"

The refrigerator was full of vegetables.

It was just like the produce section at the grocery store. It's too early for broccoli or celery or sweet potatoes, Abby thought to herself. She pulled open one of the crisper drawers and found apples and tangerines and oranges.

"Fruit salad!" she said triumphantly. She filled her arms and shut the fridge door with her foot. Then she unloaded the fruit onto the countertop and searched for a bowl and a sharp knife.

"Got it," announced Tess, returning with a level scoop of dried pellets.

"Good," said Abby. "Put it in her dish and then give her fresh water."

Prissy started eating even before Tess had finished dumping the food into her dish. Giggling, Tess picked up the water dish and carried it to the sink. By the time she returned, the dried food was almost gone.

Abby sliced the tangerines and oranges and dropped them into a large bowl. Next she added chopped apple, banana slices and green grapes. Stirring the mixture with a wooden spoon, she surveyed it with pride. It looked delicious. She popped a piece of apple into her mouth and crunched it loudly.

"Yum," said Tess as she swiped a grape.

"Okay, okay. Let's leave some for Prissy," Abby said. She set the bowl on the floor. Prissy honked happily and began devouring the fresh fruit.

"I see why they're called pigs," Abby said with a wry smile. Prissy ate rapidly, smacking her lips and chewing with her mouth wide open. They watched her gobble up every last bite. Then she slurped her water. When she was done, she stared up at them expectantly.

"No more," laughed Abby. "You've got to watch your weight, remember?"

Prissy looked disappointed.

"Can we go outside and play now?" begged Tess.

"That's a good idea," said Abby. Sunshine streamed in through the garden doors. "You two go ahead. I'll clean up."

Tess yipped happily and flung open the

doors. Fresh air flooded the kitchen, bringing with it the sound of birds singing and the scent of newly mown grass. Tess and Prissy raced outside.

Abby picked up the fruit salad bowl and carried it to the sink. After rinsing it with hot water she turned it upside down in the sink to drip dry. She'd probably use it tomorrow when it came time to feed Prissy again.

Mentally, she ran through Ms. Fitzpatrick's checklist. Prissy had been given food and water. Tess was playing with her. What was next?

Oh yeah, she remembered without enthusiasm. She had to empty the litter box.

9 Prissy Takes a Stand

With a sigh, Abby headed to Prissy's room. Tess had left the food bag wide open, so Abby closed it. She knelt on the carpet by the wicker basket and straightened the quilt. She picked up the toys and arranged them neatly. Soon the room was nice and tidy.

She couldn't put it off any longer. It was time to deal with the litter box.

Ms. Fitzpatrick had explained exactly how to do it. Abby pulled on a pair of rubber gloves and picked up the box by its handle. It was fairly light, but whatever was inside shifted against the plastic sides.

Abby grimaced. She held the litter box as far away from her body as possible and walked quickly to the backyard.

"Ew, gross!" Tess gave a yelp and high-tailed it to the opposite end of the yard.

Abby kept walking. Some help Tess was. Tomorrow she would make her do the litter box.

When she reached the garbage can she realized she'd been holding her breath. She let it out with a big *WHOOSH*.

She returned the empty litter box to its spot and refilled it with kitty litter. Then she hurried to the bathroom to wash the gloves and hang them up to dry.

"I'm glad that's over with," she said out loud. She glanced at her watch. Half an hour left. Just long enough for a little quality time with Prissy.

But what did pot-bellies like to do? She'd feel dumb rolling around in the grass with her like Tess did. Maybe she could set up the plastic bowling pins and they could play a game. Wait a minute. This was pet-sitting, not baby-sitting.

The bottles in Prissy's bedroom cupboard caught her eye. "Papaya shampoo, mango moisturizing lotion . . ." she read out loud. What great fruity names. They gave her an idea.

Abby grabbed the bottles and headed outside. She spotted Tess and Prissy in the sandbox. Tess was digging a hole with her hands and

Prissy was helping with her snout. They were both covered in sand.

Perfect, Abby thought to herself. Armed with her fragrant potions, she marched over to the sandbox.

"Wanna help?" asked Tess. She shook some sand out of her hair.

"Nope," said Abby. "It's bath time. Go get the hose."

"Yippee," shouted Tess. She raced for the hose, which lay in a coil at the corner of the house. Holding the nozzle like a weapon, she squeezed the trigger.

Abby got hit in the shoulder. "Point it at the pool, Tess!" She jumped aside as another stream of water shot her way. "Hey," she yelled. "We're here to work, not play."

"Sorry," giggled Tess. She pointed the hose at the wading pool.

While the pool was filling Abby slipped into the house to find something to dry Prissy with. She hesitated in the bathroom. All the towels were thick and fluffy. Would she get into trouble if she used one for Prissy? She thought of the pig's fancy room and soft quilt, then grabbed the prettiest towel in the pile.

Abby tossed the towel on the grass beside the pool and went to turn off the water. Everything was ready. Except for one thing.

"Where's Prissy?" she asked Tess. She tried to ignore a sudden twinge of anxiety.

"She was here a minute ago," Tess answered. She shrugged. "Maybe she doesn't want to take a bath."

"Come on," said Abby. "How would she know what we're doing?"

"She's pretty smart," Tess said. "She saw the shampoo bottle and the pool filling with water. I bet she's hiding."

"Don't be ridiculous," snapped Abby. "You act like she's a person or something. She's just a pig, for crying out loud." She was starting to get a little fed up. Abby was in charge, not Prissy. And whether she liked it or not, Prissy was going to have a bath.

"I'm glad Prissy didn't hear you say that,"

grumbled Tess. She folded her arms across her chest and glared at her sister.

"Prissy," called Abby. "It's time for a bath."

"Don't say that word," insisted Tess. "She doesn't like baths. She might get mad at you."

"Prissy, bath time!" Abby called louder. "Come on girl, where are you?"

There was no answering honk. Abby and Tess searched the yard, but Prissy was gone.

"This isn't working," said Abby at last. She tried to think. There was nothing about this in her notes. She needed to tempt Prissy out of hiding. She needed something irresistible.

Food, Abby thought. That was it. "I need bait," she announced to Tess.

Inside the kitchen something crunched beneath her shoe. It was sand. A trail of sand led across the linoleum floor straight to Prissy's bedroom door.

"Ah ha," cried Abby. "I know where you are!"

Just as she expected, Prissy was in her basket, her head thrust under the quilt Abby had arranged so neatly. The rest of her body was fully visible. Her tail quivered when Abby said her name, but she kept her head stubbornly hidden.

Abby sat down beside the basket. She scratched behind Prissy's ears the way she'd seen Tess do it. Prissy's skin felt surprisingly pleasant. She had a fine coat of hair that was soft under Abby's fingers. Abby scratched some more and Prissy seemed to relax. Slowly the piglet pulled her head out from under the quilt.

"That's right," said Abby in a soothing voice. "There's nothing to be afraid of. We're just going to have a nice, sudsy bath."

10 Breakfast Cereal Surprise

As soon as Abby said the word "bath," Prissy jerked away and shoved her head back under the quilt. Abby bit her lip. It looked like Tess was right. Bath must be one of the fifteen words Prissy knew, and it obviously wasn't one of her favorites.

It took several minutes of scratching before Prissy could be coaxed out again. This time Abby was careful not to say the "B" word. Instead she talked to Prissy about things she thought pigs might like. Abby didn't know if the words "mud puddle" and "all-you-can-eat buffet" were in Prissy's vocabulary, but they seemed to relax her.

Wrapping her arms around Prissy's pudgy middle, Abby hoisted her up and headed outdoors. For a piglet who wasn't quite three months old, she sure was heavy. Abby's arms were ready to fall off by the time she collapsed with Prissy on the grass beside the wading pool.

"Ugh," she gasped. "Watch her for a minute, will you Tess? I've got to catch my breath."

Prissy sat with her back to the pool. She wouldn't even look at the water.

"Okay, let's get this, um, b-a-t-h over with." Abby felt silly spelling out a word so Prissy wouldn't understand it, but she wasn't taking any chances.

Try as they might, they couldn't get Prissy into the pool. They pushed her, pulled her, begged her and cajoled her. Nothing worked. Prissy dug in her heels and refused to move.

Abby was really sweating now. The cold, clear water was awfully inviting. Prissy must be hot too, she thought. There was nothing in her research about pot-bellies being afraid of water. In fact, on hot days, splashing in the water was recommended so they wouldn't overheat. What was wrong with Prissy?

"Forget it," Abby said finally. "This isn't going to work. I thought it'd be fun to give her a bath, but . . ."

Suddenly a thought occurred to her. She knew just the person to call! Grandma Ida would know exactly what to do. Abby ran inside to the phone.

"Hello?" came Grandma Ida's familiar voice over the line.

"Hi Gran, it's me," said Abby. Without wasting any time, she launched right into the problem. "So do you have any ideas?" she asked when she had finished.

Grandma Ida chuckled. "The pigs around here don't have pools. Although I do know a lady who gives her prize-winning hog a milk bath before taking it to the local fair. I could give her a call . . . ."

The garden doors banged open and Tess flew into the kitchen. Ignoring Abby, she started rummaging through the cupboards.

"Woof!" she cried, seizing a box of cereal. Then she disappeared through the doors.

"Uh, gotta go, Gran," Abby said hastily. "Thanks anyway."

Abby ran after her. "Tess! Just what do

you think you're doing?"

"Watch," said Tess, plopping down on the grass beside Prissy. First she let her sniff the box. Next she shook a couple of cereal "O"s into her hand and held it under Prissy's snout. Prissy gobbled them up. Then, before Abby could stop her, she poured the whole box into the wading pool. Within seconds the pool looked like a giant bowl of breakfast cereal.

"Hey," protested Abby. "You're making a mess!"

"Wait," Tess told her.

Prissy eyed the wading pool, then inched forward for a closer look. The "O"s floated

temptingly on the surface of the water. Throwing a defiant look at Abby, Prissy stepped into the pool.

"Yippee!" cried Tess. She threw back her head and howled with delight.

Prissy plunged her snout into the water and began scooping up the soggy bits of food. This was Abby's chance. She grabbed the shampoo and a soft-bristled brush and quickly scrubbed her back, belly and legs. By the time the last "O" had disappeared, the bath was over.

Abby heaved Prissy out of the pool and held her firmly while Tess used the hose to rinse off bits of cereal that had stuck to her skin. Then Abby dried her with the towel. Finally they rubbed mango moisturizer into her skin. Prissy grunted contentedly.

By the time they got Prissy safely back in the house and the yard cleaned up, the hour they had meant to spend with her had turned into two.

Abby locked the front door and walked

home beside Tess. Her wet clothes clung uncomfortably to her stomach and legs, her arms ached from carrying Prissy and she smelled of papaya, mango and breakfast cereal.

But in spite of it all, she couldn't wait to go back tomorrow!

11 After the Hurricane

When Abby and Tess arrived at Ms. Fitzpatrick's the next morning the first thing Abby noticed was the mess.

The living room looked like it had been hit by a hurricane. Toys were scattered everywhere, as usual, but what caught Abby's eye was the rest of the room. Pillows had been thrown off the sofa and chairs, vases and knick-knacks had been knocked over and small tables lay overturned on the floor. It was a disaster area.

"What happened in here?" asked Tess, staring wide-eyed at the chaos.

"I don't know," said Abby, looking around in dismay. "We sure didn't leave it like this."

Tentatively they stepped through the room. Suddenly Abby stopped in her tracks. "Listen," she whispered.

Voices, laughter, music.

"The TV is on again. I know I turned it off yesterday."

Tess stared at her sister anxiously. "Do you think it's robbers for real this time?"

Abby shrugged. It didn't seem likely, but what else would explain the ransacked living room? And televisions don't just turn themselves on.

"Prissy!" whimpered Tess. "We have to find her!"

Abby knew she'd never get Tess out of the house if she thought Prissy was in danger. There was no point in even asking her to leave. Tess could be as stubborn as a bulldog.

"Fine," Abby whispered. "But stay with me, okay?"

Tess nodded. Holding hands, they inched toward the kitchen. It was empty. So was Prissy's room. All they could hear was the sound of the television floating down the stairs from Ms. Fitzpatrick's bedroom.

They crept up the stairs.

". . . over high heat to ensure even flavor," came the cheerful voice of the cooking show host. "If you slice your vegetables beforehand, you'll speed your preparation time."

Abby and Tess exchanged glances. What kind of criminal watched a cooking show? They climbed the last few steps and tiptoed across the landing to the bedroom door.

Nobody was there except the TV chef, who was stir-frying something in a wok. The sound of sizzling filled the room. A delighted honk came from the four-poster bed.

Abby and Tess stared at the bed. Right in the middle, almost covered by pillows, lay Prissy. She barked a greeting.

"This must be her favorite show," giggled Tess. "It's all about food!"

"Yeah, but how did the TV get turned on?" demanded Abby. "Prissy's pretty smart, I'll admit that, but she's way too short to reach the power button. Somebody else turned the TV on, somebody who wasn't supposed to be here."

Tess leapt up on the bed beside Prissy. They barked happily at each other, then settled back to watch the chef prepare a plate of long, thin noodles.

"Maybe it was a ghost," suggested Tess. She seemed to be excited by the thought.

"There are no such things as ghosts," Abby said automatically. "There has to be a rational explanation."

Maybe there had been a power surge, thought Abby. Sometimes they got power surges at home in the apartment and the electricity would blink on and off.

She looked at the phone on Ms. Fitzpatrick's night table. If there had been a break-in, she had to call someone. But if she called the police and it turned out to be a power surge, she'd feel pretty stupid. And if she called Mom and Dad, they might not let her come back and finish the job. And Prissy would have to go to the kennel.

Ms. Fitzpatrick was counting on her. Prissy was counting on her.

"Let's go make breakfast," Abby said at last. She still hadn't decided what to do, but there was no point in letting Prissy go hungry while she figured it out.

Prissy jumped from the bed to the footstool to the floor. Her stubby legs were a blur of motion as she trotted ahead of them down the stairs. By the time Abby and Tess got to the kitchen, Prissy was waiting for them by her food dish. Tess went to get the dried food while Abby checked the refrigerator.

"Don't forget to close the bag this time," Abby shouted absently. Her mind was still on the TV. A power surge might explain how the television suddenly turned itself on, but what about the disaster in the living room? A power surge couldn't have done that.

Abby set a head of cauliflower and some broccoli florets on the counter. Could Prissy have made the mess herself? Maybe she'd been angry about being left alone and had had a temper tantrum. Or maybe she'd been upset because of the bath.

Was it possible?

12 Abby's Dilemma

Abby chopped the vegetables and put them into the bowl. Her gaze wandered to the phone. Should she call someone?

Prissy made short work of the vegetables, then turned her attention to the pellets and her water dish. When she was done she let out a noise that sounded suspiciously like a burp.

I'd better phone Mom and Dad, Abby thought reluctantly. She walked into the living room and looked around, wishing she didn't have to make the call.

Just then Prissy barreled past. Using her snout as a lever, she tipped over a potted plant. Dirt spilled onto the carpet and Prissy snuffled through the plant's roots.

"Prissy's still mad," said Tess. "I told you she didn't like baths."

Abby stared at the piglet, speechless. Prissy snorted and marched over to a small table that held a set of tiny porcelain figurines.

Grunting, she nudged the base of the table with her head, causing it to rock wildly.

Tess ran over to steady it. "See?"

"You think she did all this just because she was upset?" Abby asked.

Thud! Thud! Thud! Prissy was butting her head against the leg of the coffee table.

"Okay, okay," cried Abby. She pulled Prissy away from the furniture and scratched her behind the ears to calm her down. "Prissy must have had a tempter tantrum. I guess it would be silly to call the police just to report a mess."

"Woof!" agreed Tess. "Let's play outside!"

"Let's clean up first," Abby said, glaring at her sister. "And not the way you do it at home, either. Properly this time."

Tess groaned. Even Prissy looked disappointed. But Abby held firm. "You pick things up," she said. "I'll see if I can find the vacuum."

Soon the living room was back to normal. Squealing with delight, Tess and Prissy raced outside. Abby decided to rinse out the food bowl. Just as she was leaving the kitchen, she noticed the microwave.

If a freak power surge had turned on the television, then why weren't the clock numbers on the microwave blinking?

Abby thought about the mysterious television that turned itself on every morning. How was it possible? Someone must be sneaking into the house at night. But that didn't make any sense. What kind of a prowler snuck into a house to watch the TV instead of steal it?

It also bothered Abby that Ms. Fitzpatrick's privacy had been invaded. Abby knew how important privacy was. Sharing a bedroom with Tess was fun, but it meant she was hardly ever alone. And she needed to be alone to write in her super-secret diary. She kept it hidden in the very back of her desk drawer. Even Tess didn't know about it. Sometimes, when she was desperate, she'd sneak the diary into the bathroom to write in it there. It was the only room in the apartment with a lock.

It wasn't that she didn't trust Tess, it was just that some things were private. To be certain that Tess didn't find the diary and read it, Abby had a secret way of telling if it had been tampered with. It was a trick she'd learned from Rachel, who had two nosy brothers.

The trick went like this: When Abby was done writing she carefully placed a piece of thread on one of the pages. If the diary was opened, the thread would fall out. Because Abby knew exactly where she'd put the thread, she could tell if it had been put back in the wrong spot. Actually, she'd never had a chance to find out if the trick worked, but Rachel had sworn it was foolproof.

Abby bit her lip, thinking hard. Why couldn't she do the same thing with Ms. Fitzpatrick's house? She found Tess in the backyard, playing a game of toss-the-beach-ball with Prissy.

"Hey," she said. "I need your help."

"With what?"

"You'll see," Abby said excitedly. "We're going to solve this mystery once and for all!"

13 The Booby Trap

"Solve the mystery?" repeated Tess. She stared at Abby. "How?"

Abby lowered her voice dramatically. "Booby trap," she said.

Tess scratched behind her left ear, puzzled. "You want to booby trap a ghost?"

"No," sighed Abby. "A real live human being. The prowler. Come on, I need a few things."

"Okay," said Tess agreeably. "I think Prissy needs a nap anyway."

They tucked Prissy into her sleeping basket. Playing with Tess must have worn her out because her eyes were closed even before they left the room.

"There are two doors to this house," said Abby, thinking her plan through step by step. "The garden doors in the kitchen and the front door on the verandah. We'll need to booby trap them both."

"Woof," replied Tess, eager to help.

Together they gathered the equipment they would need. Abby found scissors and tape on the shelf under the kitchen phone. Tess discovered a spool of white thread in one of the bathroom drawers. They carried everything outside.

Abby dragged a patio chair across the grass and set it down close to the garden doors. She snipped off a long piece of thread. Then she handed the scissors to Tess and climbed up on the chair. "Tape, please."

Tess handed up the tape. Abby tore off a short piece and used it to fasten one end of the thread to the outside of the house. Then she climbed down and surveyed her work. The tape was so clear you could hardly see it. Satisfied, she moved the chair over a bit and climbed up again.

"Thread," she ordered, holding her hand out like a surgeon calling for her instruments. Tess passed her the end of the thread that dangled from the house.

Pulling the thread taut, Abby attached it to the wall on the other side of the doors. She pressed it down firmly.

"There," she said proudly. The thread stretched straight across the tops of the two doors. It was nearly invisible in the daylight and would be impossible to see in the dark. "It's done."

"That's the booby trap?" asked Tess.

"Well, duh," said Abby. "As long as nobody opens the doors, the thread will stay exactly where you see it now. But if anyone goes in or out, snap! The thread will break and we'll have proof that someone has entered the house. It's perfect! I got the idea from . . ." Abby paused, thinking of her secret diary. "From Rachel."

"Wow," breathed Tess. She stared at the booby trap. "You're as smart as Prissy."

"Let's go do the screen door at the front," Abby said, ignoring the comparison. "And tomorrow we'll find out the truth, one way or another."

14 An Early Start

The next morning dawned sunny and warm. It felt strange to be home on a Monday. Abby was the first person up, as usual. She liked waking early, while the apartment was still and Tess lay dreaming on the other side of the bedroom.

Abby tiptoed to her desk. She looked over at Tess to make sure she was still sleeping, then took her diary out of its hiding spot and slipped back into bed. She kept an eye on her sister, ready to shove the diary under the covers if she woke up.

Carefully she opened the diary, checking to make sure the thread was where she'd left it. It was. Her secrets were still safe.

She chewed on the little gold pencil that had come with the diary and wondered about Ms. Fitzpatrick's house. What would she and Tess find when they got there today? Would the threads be intact? All of a sudden she didn't feel like writing anymore. She just had to see if the booby traps had been sprung!

Abby stuffed the diary into her drawer. She threw on shorts and a T-shirt, then took her key string off the bedpost and put it over her head. Tess mumbled and rolled over.

"Wake up," Abby whispered, leaning close to where she imagined Tess's ear to be. Tess slept all rolled up in her blankets, so it was hard to tell for sure. She rolled over again, pulling the blankets more tightly around her body.

"Come on," Abby said, raising her voice. "We have to check on Prissy." She tugged the blankets down and discovered she'd been talking to Tess's feet.

"Prissy?" repeated Tess in a groggy voice. Finally she sat up. "Okay, I'm awake."

Tess stumbled out of bed and put on the clothes Abby handed her. With her eyes half shut she followed Abby down the hall to the kitchen.

They found Dad at the stove, cooking breakfast.

"You girls are just in time," he said as Tess slumped down in her chair at the kitchen table. "Are you hungry?"

Tess didn't answer. Her eyes had closed again and she was leaning slightly to one side.

"Not really," said Abby. Who could think of food at a time like this? They had a mystery to solve! Something sure did smell good, though. "What're you making?" she asked.

Dad waved his spatula in the air. "French toast . . . with chocolate chips!"

Abby licked her lips. She loved it when her dad cooked. Mom was a good cook too, but Dad liked to try fun stuff like peanut butter waffles and butterscotch oatmeal.

"Well, I guess I could try one," she said. "But then we've got to get going. We have an important job this morning."

"The early bird gets the worm, right?" joked Dad.

Abby picked up her fork and dug into her piping hot French toast. With any luck, the early pet-sitters would get the prowler!

15 Plan B

Dad dropped the girls at Ms. Fitzpatrick's house on his way to work. Abby practically flew up the verandah steps, she was so excited. Tess wasn't far behind. What would they find? Would the booby traps be sprung? Had a prowler really broken in during the night?

The white thread was stretched across the screen door exactly as they'd left it yesterday.

"If it's a ghost," Tess said thoughtfully, "it would just float through the thread. If it's a wizard, it would cast a magic spell . . ."

"Let's check around back," said Abby, cutting her off. She didn't want to listen to a bunch of make-believe mumbo jumbo. Sometimes Tess had an overactive imagination.

In the backyard they found the same thing. The white thread was undisturbed.

"Well, that's good," Abby said, feeling oddly disappointed. "Nobody's gone in or out of the house since last night. Prissy must be safe and sound."

"Woof," cried Tess. She pawed at the garden doors, eager to see her little pink friend.

Walking slowly, Abby led Tess back to the verandah. The thread snapped soundlessly when she pulled the screen door open. She used the key around her neck to unlock the inside door.

"At least Prissy didn't have another temper tantrum," she said to Tess as they walked down the hall to the kitchen. The usual toys were scattered here and there, but everything else was in order.

Tess barked out a greeting, hoping Prissy would run to meet them. "Prissy," she called. As they neared the kitchen a familiar sound reached their ears.

Abby and Tess stared at each other in disbelief. The television was on.

But how? The booby traps hadn't been sprung. And when they'd left yesterday, they'd made double sure the TV was off.

It was impossible!

Abby ran up the stairs two at a time. She found Prissy in her favorite spot, watching the same chef in the same apron create a perfect pizza pie.

"I don't believe it," cried Abby.

"Maybe Prissy can do magic," suggested Tess uncertainly.

"She can't," snapped Abby. "I'm sure there's a perfectly reasonable explanation."

"What?"

Abby stared at Tess, wishing she could think of one. "I don't know," she cried, "but there's an explanation and it's got nothing to do with magic. I'll prove it to you!"

Abby thundered down the stairs, her mind racing. What she needed was another plan, and fast.

Tomorrow was Tuesday and Ms. Fitz-patrick was flying home at noon. If Abby was going to get to the bottom of this mystery, she had to do it soon. It was time to call in someone who was good at detective work.

"Hello?" said a sleepy voice.

Abby spoke quickly. "Rachel, I need your help. It's an emergency."

Twenty minutes later Rachel was at the door, her backpack slung over one shoulder. Abby let her in.

"Did you bring it?" she asked anxiously.

Rachel yawned and nodded. "Uh huh. Where do you want it?"

"The TV is upstairs," Abby said, eyeing the backpack. "Are you sure you know how to use it?"

"No problem," Rachel assured her. "Mom let me take it to drama class last month. I was the only one with a video camera at home."

Abby led her upstairs. The cooking show was over and Prissy was getting restless. "There's the TV," she said, pointing.

"Honk," grumbled Prissy. She jumped off the bed and prodded Abby's leg with her snout.

"I'd better feed her," Abby said to Rachel. "Can you set it up alone?"

"Sure," said Rachel, already fiddling with the cables and wires.

Prissy pushed Abby's leg again, harder this time. "Okay, okay," Abby said, bending over to scratch her behind the ear. "Let's go make breakfast."

Abby sliced some peaches and nectarines into a bowl and put it on the floor. While Prissy enjoyed her breakfast, Abby pulled on the yellow rubber gloves and took care of the litter box. It was still a gross job, but today she had other things to think about.

A magic pig. What a preposterous idea. Maybe Tess still believed in foolish stuff like magic, but Abby knew there had to be a reasonable, logical explanation for the television being on every morning.

Rachel's video camera would prove it!

16 Seeing Is Believing

When Abby's alarm rang the next morning she leapt out of bed and dressed in record time. It was set to ring a half hour earlier than usual, but she didn't feel the least bit tired. She and Tess had some unfinished business to attend to before going to school.

Grabbing her backpack, Abby kissed Mom on the cheek and headed down the apartment stairs after Tess. Rachel met them in front of Ms. Fitzpatrick's house.

"Secret agent Katz reporting for duty," Rachel said smartly.

"Very funny," said Abby, too nervous about what they might find at Ms. Fitzpatrick's to play along.

"Is Rachel coming too?" asked Tess.

"You bet," Abby answered. She strode toward the verandah. "I'm going to prove once and for all that pigs can't do magic."

People along the street were setting out

their garbage cans and bringing in their newspapers. Tess barked at the mailman, who smiled and waved back.

"Here we are," Abby said, reaching for her key string. "It's time to see what's on that tape."

Just like every other morning, the sound of the television greeted them when they walked into the kitchen. The three girls raced up the stairs. This time they found two gardeners explaining how to create a rock garden.

Abby dropped her backpack on the bedroom carpet and turned off the TV. Then she went to the bookshelf where Rachel had set up the video camera. It was partly hidden by a leafy plant.

She handed the camera to Rachel, who hooked it up to the television. Pressing the rewind button, Abby found the beginning of the video and turned the TV back on.

"Okay, guys," she said. "Watch this."

Abby pushed the start button. They could clearly see the four-poster bed, the television and the door to the hall. After a few minutes of

nothing happening, Abby hit the fast-forward button. Suddenly Prissy appeared on the screen. Still in fast-forward, she zipped across the room and flew onto the bed. Almost instantaneously the television came alive.

"Freaky," Rachel said quietly.

"What?" cried Abby. She stabbed at the stop button, then pressed rewind. Impatiently she pushed "Start."

Once more Prissy entered the room, trotting at regular speed this time. She clambered up the footstool and walked to the middle of the bed. Nosing the pillows this way and that, she took her time settling into her usual spot.

Abby leaned closer to the screen. She didn't want to miss a thing. After a minute, all by itself, the television turned on.

"Wow," breathed Tess. "Prissy can do magic." She looked at Rachel, then at her sister. "I was right!"

"That's impossible," sputtered Abby. "I don't believe it!"

"Videotape doesn't lie," said Rachel.

"Seeing is believing, isn't that what you always say?"

"She just looked at the TV and it came on," whispered Tess. "She's got powers."

"Powers schmowers," said Abby. This was crazy. No matter what it looked like on videotape, she wasn't going to believe that Prissy had special powers. Frustrated, she kicked her backpack.

Tess began to dance around the room. "Prissy has powers, Prissy has powers," she chanted. She barked excitedly and clambered up the footstool and onto the bed. Giggling, she plopped down in Prissy's favorite spot.

The TV went blank.

Abby stared at it, flabbergasted. Her mind whirled. Maybe it wasn't the pig who had powers. Maybe it was the bed. Or maybe it was something on the bed. Pushing Tess aside, she began tossing the fancy pillows right and left.

"What are you doing?" cried Rachel, rescuing a pillow shaped like a sausage.

"Ah ha!" shouted Abby. She held her arm

in the air triumphantly. “I found it!”

Rachel and Tess stared at her.

“What is it?” asked Tess timidly.

“The remote!” cried Abby. She waved the black rectangular object in the air. “Prissy was sitting on the remote control the whole time. Whenever she sat in her spot, the remote would turn the TV on. I knew there was a perfectly logical explanation. I just knew it!”

Prissy appeared in the doorway, awakened by the commotion. She grunted hungrily and climbed onto the bed. Tess gave her a big hug. “Well, I still think Prissy can do magic.”

Abby stared at her. “Huh?”

Tess grinned. “She sure can make food disappear!”

17 Abby Learns a Lesson

Rachel packed the video camera in its case and they hurried to school so they wouldn't be late. Abby felt good all day. Once again, clear-headed reasoning and cold, hard facts had prevailed.

After school Abby and Tess returned to Ms. Fitzpatrick's to get paid.

"Thank you both for doing such a great job," said Ms. Fitzpatrick after she'd ushered them into the living room. "Prissy was so content when I got home today."

"She's a very smart pig," Abby said with a smile.

Ms. Fitzpatrick scooped Prissy into her arms and cuddled her. "Yes, she is," she crooned. "Mommy's little girl is the smartest piggy in the whole wide world, right, sweetie?"

Prissy wiggled with delight.

"What's that?" asked Tess, pointing to something that was sparkling around Prissy's neck.

"I always buy my baby a little present when I go on a trip," Ms. Fitzpatrick explained. She tilted up Prissy's chin so they could get a better look. It was a collar made of shiny pink rhinestones. A dainty heart hung down from the front.

Abby leaned closer. A word was engraved in the center of the heart. "Prissy," she read out loud.

"That must have cost a lot," Tess blurted out.

"Nothing's too good for my baby," said Ms. Fitzpatrick, setting Prissy down. Prissy grunted and sat back on her haunches. She looked from Abby to Tess, then back to Abby again. If Abby didn't know better, she'd swear Prissy winked at her.

"That reminds me," Abby said, reaching for the string around her neck. "Here's your key back. Give us a call if you ever need our help again."

Ms. Fitzpatrick took the key from Abby and handed her an envelope. "Here's something for you too."

"Thanks," Abby said politely, tucking it into her backpack.

"Thanks a whole bunch," Tess added with a grin. She followed her sister to the front door.

"Actually," said Ms. Fitzpatrick. "I would prefer if you opened it now."

Abby paused, then pulled the envelope out again. Wasn't it rude to count money in front of a customer? "Uh, okay."

The flap wasn't glued shut so Abby was able to open it easily. She pulled out a check. But something else was in the envelope too. It was a card. The front was decorated with balloons and party hats, and in the center were the words, "You are invited!" With a surprised glance at Tess, she opened the card.

"Come celebrate Prissy's birthday," she read out loud.

Ms. Fitzpatrick beamed. "Prissy's going to be three months old and we're having a party. I know she would love you to be there. It will be such fun. I've hired a clown and the food is being catered by Prissy's favorite restaurant . . . you'll come, of course."

"Uh, okay," said Abby, not entirely sure she wanted to go to a pig's birthday party.

Tess had no such doubts. "Woof," she barked enthusiastically. "Birthday cake!"

Abby sighed. Barking, sloppiness, food . . . . Tess and Prissy sure had a lot in common.

"Wonderful," declared Ms. Fitzpatrick. She walked with them to the verandah. "Prissy has such fun at parties. She adores opening presents."

Tess ran ahead to the sidewalk, but Abby hung back. There was something she needed to find out.

"Ms. Fitzpatrick," she said hesitantly, "can I ask you something? You're a computer programmer, and, well . . . why do you treat Prissy like a kid? I mean, she's a nice pig, but . . ."

Ms. Fitzpatrick laughed. "You're wondering why someone like me would be so crazy about a pet? It's simple, really. At work I'm surrounded by codes and programs and factual

information. It's all very real and orderly. And all very boring. Prissy lets me relax. Not everything has to be logical, you know. Sometimes a little silliness can be good for you."

Abby thought about Ms. Fitzpatrick's words while she and Tess washed the supper dishes that night. Was she right? Was silliness good? Maybe I'm getting boring, Abby thought.

"There's going to be a clown," Tess was

saying to Mom excitedly. She gave her plate a quick swipe with a tea towel. "Maybe he'll do tricks and stuff. I can't wait!"

"I didn't realize pigs celebrated birthdays," Mom said, taking Tess's plate and drying it properly. "Are you going, Abby?"

"Abby won't go! She probably thinks it's too crazy," declared Tess. "I want to wear my polka-dot dress. It's pink, and that's Prissy's favorite color. Or maybe I'll wear my new jumper with the strawberries all over it, because Prissy loves food. Or maybe . . ."

"I think you've got a bigger problem than deciding what to wear," interrupted Abby.

"You're not going to start talking about logic, are you?" asked Tess with a grimace.

Abby flicked her with the soapy dishcloth and smiled. "Nope. I was just wondering what kind of present we should buy for a pig who has everything."